Sprinkle Your Sparkles

Show Your Love and Kindness

Written by
Kirsten Tulsian

Illustrated by
Mary Gregg Byrne

FERNE PRESS

Sprinkle Your Sparkles: Show Your Love and Kindness

Copyright © 2013 by Kirsten Walgren Tulsian

Layout and cover design by Jacqueline L. Challiss Hill
Illustrations by Mary Gregg Byrne
Illustrations created with watercolors

Printed in the United States of America

Summary: Children and others spread love and kindness with their inner sparkles.

Library of Congress Cataloging-in-Publication Data
    Tulsian, Kirsten Walgren
    Sprinkle Your Sparkles: Show Your Love and Kindness/Kirsten Walgren Tulsian–First Edition
    ISBN-13: 978-1-938326-20-2
    1. Juvenile fiction. 2. Feelings and emotions. 3. Unselfishness. 4. Empathy.
    I. Tulsian, Kirsten Walgren II. Title
    Library of Congress Control Number: 2013947959

FERNE PRESS

Ferne Press is an imprint of Nelson Publishing & Marketing
366 Welch Road, Northville, MI 48167
www.nelsonpublishingandmarketing.com
(248) 735-0418

Dedication

Dedicated to my loves, Kai and Ella.
The sparkles you sprinkle shine to the moon
and back to infinity!

You have a deep pocket that rests by your chest,
filled with love, boundless passion, and glorious zest.

If you peeked right inside this deep pocket of yours,
you'd be mesmerized by the amount that it stores.

These magnificent pebbles of boundless bright white
are called sparkles, of course,

for they are divine light.

Dear one, oh, Dear one,
open your eyes
to see that there's plenty,
an endless supply.

7

From here to eternity, beyond this planet we treasure, your pocket stays filled for this fantastic adventure.

8

At any old moment, with all of your might,
grab a handful of sparkles and toss with delight.

9

Imagine their brilliance, their sheer and pure light,
as you share them aplenty with all in your sight.

Use sparkles for gratitude to say, "I thank you,"
for all that you are and all that you do.

When the sun rises in the morning or sets at night,
give thanks for the love that flows into your life.

Sprinkle your sparkles of love and light;
make your beauty shine endlessly bright!

Use sparkles for forgiveness to say, "Please forgive me," for hurts that were caused to show that you're sorry.

When feelings get hurt or an accident happens,
mend the mistake with grace, love, and passion.

Sprinkle your sparkles of love and light;
make your beauty shine endlessly bright!

Use sparkles for healing to say, "I hope you get well,"
for all those around you, to help them feel swell.

16

When someone feels pain, sadness, or hurt,
relief is the goal that we must support.

Sprinkle your sparkles of
love and light; make your beauty
shine endlessly bright!

Use sparkles for love to say, "I love you,"
for the sheer adoration, the passion that's true.

When bliss is the direction,
the destiny you create,
love will abound, it's nature's soul mate.

Sprinkle your sparkles
of love and light;
make your beauty
shine endlessly bright!

Use sparkles for harmony to say,
"I choose peace,"
for the love and kindness to always increase.

20

When situations in life call for resolution,
choose the nonviolent, most peaceful solution.

Sprinkle your sparkles of love and light;
make your beauty shine endlessly bright!

When you grab all those sparkles
and share them in surplus,

your beauty and love shine with great purpose.

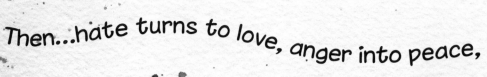

Then...hate turns to love, anger into peace,

frustration
becomes contentment,
when sparkles release.

Every single second, it's your choice to make,

use the love inside you to create a sparkle-lit place.

24

The energy you put out there makes a difference to the rest,

like ripples in a pond, it journeys north, south, east, and west.

Now, what are you waiting for?

Go ahead and try,
reach inside that pocket,
through your mind's eye.

26

Release them and toss them, give them a shake.
They are magnificent energy, for everyone's sake.

You can do it alone or in the company of many.
Just picture yourself throwing sparkles aplenty.

Can you even begin to imagine a place
filled with light, hope, and love,
things we all can embrace?

Your world would be lit, so magical and bright,
full of love and compassion for all things in sight.

Gratitude, forgiveness...
healing, love, and peace...
the world WILL be better for it,
share your sparkles with ease!

When you share heaps of sparkles with
all of your might,
they come back in full force from
everywhere in sight.

30

Author Letter

Dear Reader,

As a parent, caregiver, or educator, it is important to use re-inforcement and to live by example. You can encourage your children to show how they care by being aware of their surroundings and understanding that we're all connected. One of my favorite examples occurs while driving in the car with my children. Each time we pass an automobile accident, we sprinkle sparkles of love on all of the people affected by the accident, including the emergency responders. I believe our sparkles carry love and healing around the scene, and sharing them inadvertently creates a connected, empathetic, and loving response in my children. Sharing their sparkles is the best gift that they can give to the world around them, and as an added bonus, it also brings more sparkles to their own lives.

Sparkles are just like little pebbles of love that you carry with you wherever you go. You can share these sparkles just like you share your favorite toys. Sprinkle your sparkles around family, friends, pets, your neighborhood, and even the world. When you toss your sparkles of love, you make the world a better place to live. Imagine your sparkles, colorful and bright, spreading love anywhere you like!

Author Bio

Kirsten Walgren Tulsian is a mom, elementary school teacher, counselor, writer, and Reiki Master. She is passionate about uncovering magic in the world, purpose in the human experience, and the radiant light inherent in all. Her love of children, coupled with her desire to teach the world about the power of selfless compassion, resulted in the creation of *Sprinkle Your Sparkles: Show Your Love and Kindness.* For more information about Kirsten, please visit kirstentulsian.com.

Illustrator Bio

Mary Gregg Byrne lives in Bellingham, Washington. She reads, writes, and creates art. Mary teaches watercolor classes and illustrates children's books. She watches her garden and the children grow. She walks in the mountains. She cherishes her friends. Mary enjoys the changing light of the seasons and of her life. For more information about Mary and her art, please visit www.marygreggbyrne.com.